EGMONT

We bring stories to life

First published in Great Britain in 2006 by Dean,
an imprint of Egmont UK Limited
239 Kensington High Street, London W8 6SA

Thomas the Tank Engine & Friends™

A BRITT ALLCROFT COMPANY PRODUCTION

Based on The Railway Series by The Reverend W Awdry
Photographs © 2006 Gullane (Thomas) LLC. A HIT Entertainment Company

Thomas the Tank Engine & Friends and Thomas & Friends are trademarks of Gullane (Thomas) Limited.
Thomas the Tank Engine & Friends and Design is Reg. US. Pat. & Tm. Off.

ISBN 978 0 6035 6235 8
ISBN 0 6035 6235 3
3 5 7 9 10 8 6 4 2
Printed in Singapore

Percy and the Haunted Mine

The Thomas TV Series

DEAN

It was summertime on the Island of Sodor.

The Stationmasters and their staff decided to have a friendly competition to find out which was 'The Most Beautiful Station'.

They decorated all the stations with shrubs, flowers and hanging baskets.

The engines loved helping, too!

One night, The Fat Controller came to the sheds to talk to the engines.

"I want Percy to collect some shrubs to decorate Lower Tidmouth Station," he said. "They're at Maithwaite."

Percy looked scared. "Y . . . yes Sir," he said nervously.

None of the engines liked going to Maithwaite at night. They had to pass the old quarry mine. Nobody worked there any more. It was very spooky!

It was a very foggy night. Percy had his light on, but he was still a little scared.

Percy soon reached the old mine. The signal was red and he had to stop.

Suddenly, the old factory chimney started to sink into the ground!

"Bouncing buffers!" cried Percy.

When the signal changed,
Percy was so scared he
sped off as fast as he could!

The next day Percy told Donald and Douglas about the disappearing chimney.

"It's the naughty gnomes!" teased Donald.

"Little fat men with big feet. They make strange things happen," said Douglas.

"It's true! They steal your wheels!" said Donald as they chuffed away.

Percy didn't want to believe them, but he felt very scared.

That night, The Fat Controller sent Percy to collect some trucks. They were at a siding near the old quarry mine.

Percy hoped he wouldn't see anything else disappear. He slipped into the siding and buffered up to the trucks. Then he heard a strange noise.

"What's that?" said his Driver.

Suddenly, a building at the old mine sank into the ground!

"Double bouncing buffers!" shouted Percy. He was so scared, he lurched forwards and hit a truck. Its load spilled out on to the siding. There were gnomes everywhere!

"It's the naughty gnomes!" cried Percy.

He hurried away as fast as his wheels could carry him.

Back at the station, Percy's Driver told The Fat Controller that they had seen a building sink right into the ground.

"It's the naughty gnomes," said Percy, nervously. "They like to cause trouble!"

"Nonsense," said The Fat Controller. "The buildings are sinking into old mine shafts, that's all."

"But I saw the gnomes!" said Percy.

"Of course you did," smiled the Fat Controller. "They're garden gnomes! We are going to use them to decorate the station. They're not scary. They're supposed to bring good luck."

The Fat Controller ordered Percy to go back and get them. Percy didn't dare to argue.

The way to the old mine was misty and Percy was scared, but he knew he had to carry on. "I'm not afraid . . . I'm not afraid," he said to himself.

When he reached the siding, he saw the gnomes lying around on the ground. Percy waited for something spooky to happen. But it didn't.

The Fat Controller was right. The gnomes weren't scary at all!

The Driver and the Fireman collected the gnomes. Percy took them straight back to Lower Tidmouth Station.

Next day, the workmen decorated the station ready for the competition.

When the judges saw the gnomes, they said Lower Tidmouth Station was the winner!

The Stationmaster thanked Percy. "We wouldn't have won the competition without our gnomes," he said.

Percy was very proud. "You were right, Sir," he said to The Fat Controller. "Naughty gnomes can be lucky after all!"